Little Otter Remembers

AND
OTHER STORIES

By **Ann Tompert**

Pictures by **John Wallner**

Crown Publishers, Inc., New York

Text copyright © 1977 by Ann Tompert
Illustrations copyright © 1977 by John Wallner
All rights reserved. No part of this publication may be reproduced, stored in a retrieval system, or transmitted, in any form or by any means, electronic, mechanical, photocopying, recording, or otherwise, without prior written permission of the publisher. Inquiries should be addressed to Crown Publishers, Inc., One Park Avenue, New York, N.Y. 10016 : Manufactured in the United States of America : Published simultaneously in Canada by General Publishing Company Limited
10   9   8   7   6   5   4   3   2   1

The text of this book is set in 18 point Bookman. The illustrations are pre-separated pencil drawings prepared by the artist and printed in three colors.

Library of Congress Cataloging in Publication Data
Tompert, Ann.
    Little Otter's adventures.
    Summary: Little Otter selects a gift for Mother
Otter, searches for his pine cone, and attends a coasting
party with his relatives.
    [1. Otters—Fiction]   I.   Wallner, John C.   II.   Title.
PZ7.T598Ll   [E]   77-2649
ISBN 0-517-52751-0

CONTENTS

Little Otter's Birthday Gift

Little Otter hurried toward the river.
"It is Mother Otter's birthday,"
he said. "I will catch her a fish.
Mother Otter likes fish."

Little Otter jumped into the river
and swam under the water.

He saw a big fish.

"That fish is too big," he said,

and he swam deeper into the water.

There he saw a little fish.

Round and round it he swam.

"That fish is too little."

He looked and looked.

At last he saw a fish

that was just the right size.

He swam down after it, and
catching it in his mouth,
he rose to the top of the water.

Then he climbed onto the bank
of the river. He was looking
for a place to rest when
he saw a shell near a log.
"What a pretty shell," he said.
He put down the fish and
picked up the shell.
He turned it over and over.

"Maybe Mother Otter would like

a shell better than a fish.

She can catch a fish

any time she wants,

but she may never find a shell

as pretty as this."

He picked up the fish and

threw it into the river.

Then he put the shell

into his pocket

and started for home.

Along the way, he came
to a field of dandelions.
"Oh!" cried Little Otter.
"What beautiful dandelions!
Mother Otter likes dandelions."
Little Otter took the shell
out of his pocket and
turned it over and over.

"Mother Otter has lots of shells,"
said Little Otter.
"I bet she already has one like this.
I can always find her
a pretty shell, but the
flowers will soon be gone."

So Little Otter threw the shell away
and picked a fine bunch of dandelions.
Once again Little Otter
started for home.
He had not gone very far
when he came upon a

patch of blueberry bushes.

There was nothing that Little Otter

liked better than blueberries.

"I know I must get home," he said,

"but it won't hurt to eat just one."

Little Otter put the flowers
under a tree and hurried
to a blueberry bush.
He picked one berry and ate it.
It was plump and sweet
and tasted so good
that he ate another one.
Then he ate a third
and a fourth and a fifth.

Little Otter went from bush to bush,
picking and eating blueberries.
Soon great gusts of wind
tossed the bushes about,
but that did not stop him.

He was deep into the patch
when he heard someone calling,
"Little Otter! Little Otter!
Where are you?"
Peering around the bushes,
Little Otter saw his mother.
He worked his way
through the blueberry patch
to join her.

"Where have you been?"
asked Mother Otter.
"I have been looking everywhere
for you. It is going to rain.
Can't you smell it in the wind?"

"I'm sorry," said Little Otter,

"but I went to the river

to catch a fish

for your birthday."

Mother Otter put her arm around him.

"I like fish," she said.

"But then I saw a pretty shell,"
said Little Otter, "and I thought,
Mother can catch a fish any time
she wants, but she may never
find such a pretty shell."

"That's true," said Mother Otter.

"So I put the fish back in the water
and picked up the pretty shell,"
said Little Otter.

"Now I will have a new shell for
my collection," said Mother Otter.
"But you won't," said Little Otter.

"On my way home,

I saw some dandelions,

and I thought, I can find

Mother Otter a pretty shell any time,

but the flowers will soon be gone.

So I threw away the shell

and picked a bunch of dandelions."

"Flowers always make me happy,"
said Mother Otter.

"But then I saw these blueberries,"
said Little Otter.

"I just had to eat some.

So I put the flowers under a tree."

Little Otter looked and looked.

He saw many trees, but he did

not see any dandelions.

Tears came into his eyes.

"The wind blew away the flowers!"

cried Little Otter.

"Now I have nothing for your

birthday."

"Don't worry," said Mother Otter

as she gave him a big hug.

"I have you."

It was almost dark,

so they set out for home.

Waiting for them when they got there
was the cake Mother Otter had baked.

28

It was beautiful, but
Little Otter felt so bad
that no matter how hard he tried
he could not eat a single piece.

Little Otter
Remembers

"It is lost!" cried Little Otter,

as he looked under the table.

"It is lost!"

"What is lost?" asked Mother Otter.

"My pine cone,"
said Little Otter.
"I put it right here
on the table yesterday.
Did you see it?"
"Yes, I saw it,"
said Mother Otter.
"What did you do with it?"
asked Little Otter.

"Nothing," said Mother Otter.

"What did *you* do with it?"

Little Otter thought and thought.

"Oh, yes, I remember now.

I showed it to Raccoon and

then I put it on my shelf."

Little Otter ran to his room,

climbed onto his bed, and

looked on the shelf above it.

"My pine cone is not here,"

he said.

"What do you think happened to it?"

asked Mother Otter.

Little Otter thought and thought.

"Oh, yes, I remember now.

I took it to the river to wash it.

I worked very hard."

"You are a very good worker,"

said Mother Otter.

She patted him gently.

"What did you do next?"

"I sat under a tree to rest,"

said Little Otter.

"Then I put it in a hole in the tree.

That's where it is," he shouted.

And he ran out the door.

Little Otter ran through the fields
as fast as he could.
At last he came to the tree
with the hole. He bent
over and looked inside.

The pine cone was not there.

"Somebody stole it,"

he shouted, and he turned around

and ran home as fast as he could.

"Mother, Mother!" he cried.

"It is gone. My pine cone is gone.

Someone has taken it."

"Are you sure?" asked his mother.

"Someone took it," shouted Little Otter.

"Stop and think," said Mother Otter

as she put her arm around him.

"Could that someone be you?"

Little Otter closed his eyes.

He thought and thought.

"Now I remember!

I did not want to get it dirty again,

and I did not want to lose it,

so I put it in a box in my drawer."

Little Otter ran into his bedroom.

He pulled out his drawer,

took out the box, and opened it.

He ran into the kitchen.

"Here it is!" he shouted.

Mother Otter hugged him.

"I'm so glad you found it," she said.

"And now it is time for bed."

"But first," said Little Otter,

"I must put my pine cone under my pillow.

I do not want to lose it again."

Little Otter flopped onto his chest
and slid down the snow-covered hill
headfirst. After a long slide,
he stopped at the foot of the hill
in a whirl of snowflakes.

Then Mother Otter slid down the hill

and landed right beside him.

"Let's do it again," said Little Otter.

"Let's," said his mother.

Mother Otter and Little Otter

slid down the hill

until it became

as smooth as glass.

"It would be fun to have a
coasting party," said Little Otter.

"I would like that," said Mother Otter,
"but who would come?"

"I will ask all my friends,"
said Little Otter.

"Good," said Mother Otter.
"You invite your friends
while I make cookies and cocoa."

Mother Otter fixed his scarf

and gave him a kiss.

Then Little Otter hurried off.

Soon he came to a tree where

Porcupine was sitting on a high branch.

Porcupine was chewing bark.

"Will you come to my coasting party?"

asked Little Otter.

"Not now," said Porcupine,

"I am busy eating."

"We are having cookies and cocoa,"
  said Little Otter.

"I do not like sweet things,"
  said Porcupine.

"Why don't you ask Badger?"

"Thank you, I will," said Little Otter.
  And he hurried off.

Soon he came to Badger's house.

He knocked at the door,

but no one answered.

Just then Fox came by.

"You are wasting your time," he said.

"Badger is sleeping.

He says it is the best way

to get through the winter."

"Oh, dear," said Little Otter.

"I wanted to invite him

to my coasting party.

Can you come?"

"I would like to," said Fox,

"but I am expected home.

Why don't you ask Woodchuck?"

"Thank you, I will," said Little Otter.

And he hurried off.

When Little Otter came
to Woodchuck's house,
he knocked at the door.
But there was no answer.
Just as he turned to leave,
Skunk opened the door.
"What do you want?"
he asked.

"Oh, dear," said Little Otter.

"I have made a mistake.

 I thought this was Woodchuck's house."

"It is," yawned Skunk.

"But I am renting a part of his house

 for the winter."

"Oh," said Little Otter.

"Is Woodchuck home?"

"Of course," said Skunk,

"but he is sleeping.

He plans to sleep until spring.

Not a bad idea if you ask me,"

he said, and he slammed the door

in Little Otter's face.

Little Otter turned to leave.

There were tears in his eyes.

"Skunk can be rude," said Raccoon who was sitting in a tree nearby.

"No one wants to come to my coasting party," said Little Otter.

"A coasting party!" cried Raccoon.
"That sounds like fun."
"Would you like to come?"
asked Little Otter.
"Yes. And we can ask
Bear to come, too."

Little Otter and Raccoon looked
for Bear in a patch of bushes.
They could not find him.
They peered into the hollow of a
tree, but he was not there.
Nor was he in the rocky cave nearby.

Clouds began to fill the sky.

It grew darker and darker.

"It is going to snow," said Raccoon.

"I do not like snow. I am

going home until it is over."

He hurried off.

A few snowflakes drifted down.

One landed on Little Otter's nose.

"I must go home, too," he said.

"I do not want Mother Otter to worry."

He started to run.

The snow fell faster and faster.

Soon Little Otter could hardly see

where he was going.

A thick white curtain of snow

fell all around him.

As Little Otter neared home,

the snow stopped falling

and the sun began to shine.

Little Otter rubbed his eyes.

He could not believe what he saw.

But it was true.

All of his uncles and cousins and aunts

were coasting on the steep hill.

"We've come to your party,"

they called.

"Hooray!" shouted Little Otter

as he hurried to join them.

Little Otter's mother and aunts

coasted down the slide twenty-six times.

Little Otter's uncles coasted

down the slide fifty-two times.

Little Otter's cousins coasted

down the slide seventy-three times.

But Little Otter was so happy

that he coasted down the slide

one hundred and forty-seven times.

JUL 17 1978

12 PEACHTREE

J
Easy

Tompert, Ann.
Little Otter remembers, and other
stories / by Ann Tompert ; pictures by
John Wallner. New York : Crown
Publishers, c1977.
64 p. : col. ill. ; 24 cm.
SUMMARY: Little Otter selects a gift
for Mother Otter, searches for his pine
cone, and attends a coasting party with
his relatives.

JUL 17 1978

I. Wallner, John C.   II. Title